D1211717

Teach Me
To Love

By Denise Brennan-Nelson

I will learn.
Teach me, okay?
Show me, show me,
show me the way!

Teach me to swing!
Teach me to climb!
I'll swing and climb
from vine to vine.

I want to hop.
Teach me to hop.
I'll hop and hop
and never stop.

Teach me to follow.
I'll watch you lead.
All these things
from you I need.

Teach me to run
with speed and grace.
I love the feel
of wind in my face.

I need to share.
Teach me to share.
Show me, show me,
what is fair.

Teach me to play!
I want to play!
Why don't we just
play all day?

Teach me to smile,
I'll smile with you!
Laughs and giggles
all day through.

Teach me how
to be a friend.
Show me how
to stretch and bend.

I'm so sleepy.
Teach me to sleep.
Off to sleep
without a peep.

I want to love.
Teach me, okay?
Show me, show me,
show me the way.

To my parents, and all parents, who show their children what love is.

—DBN

....

Denise Brennan-Nelson has written several books for children, including *Maestro Stu Saves the Zoo*, *My Momma Likes to Say*, and *He's Been a Monster All Day!*

As a national speaker, Denise encourages adults and children to tap into their imaginations to create richer, fuller lives. She also travels the country sharing her enthusiasm for reading and writing with schoolchildren and teachers.

Denise lives in Howell, Michigan with her husband, Bob, and their two daughters, Rebecca and Rachel. Find out more about Denise at www.denisebrennannelson.com.

....

Photo Credits: ©Eric Gevaert/Shutterstock Images, cover, 23; ©Tom Brakefield/Thinkstock, back cover; ©Will Davies/iStock, 1; ©Fuse/Thinkstock, 3; ©Romas_Photo/Shutterstock Images, 5; ©Somsak Sudthangtum/Thinkstock, 6; ©Karel Gallas/Shutterstock Images, 9; ©Francois van Heerden/Shutterstock Images, 10; ©dageldog/iStock, 12; ©pjmalsbury/iStock, 14, 18; ©otsphoto/Shutterstock Images, 16; ©MilousSK/Shutterstock Images, 20

Text Copyright © 2014 Denise Brennan Nelson

Sleeping Bear Press®
315 E. Eisenhower Parkway, Ste. 200
Ann Arbor, MI 48108
www.sleepingbearpress.com

Printed and bound in the United States.

10 9 8 7 6 5 4 3 2 1

Library of Congress Cataloging-in-Publication Data

Brennan-Nelson, Denise, author.
Teach me to love / by Denise Brennan Nelson.
pages cm
Summary: "Rhyming text paired with photos of adult and baby animals demonstrate playful ways parents teach their offspring to hop, fly, run, swim, and more"—Provided by the publisher.
ISBN 978-1-58536-858-7
[1. Stories in rhyme. 2. Animals—Infancy—Fiction. 3. Parental behavior in animals—Fiction. 4. Parent and child—Fiction.] I. Title.
PZ8.3.B7457Te 2014
[E]—dc23
2014004558